Lucy Livingood

The Night Owls

Farmer Del   L'il Beaky

The County Mounties

The Moon

The Sun

To get the full value of a joy you must have somebody to divide it with.
—Mark Twain

Henry Holt and Company, *Publishers since 1866*
Henry Holt® is a registered trademark of Macmillan Publishing Group, LLC
120 Broadway, New York, NY 10271 • mackids.com

Library of Congress Cataloging-in-Publication Data
Names: Long, Ethan, author, illustrator. | Title: Sun and Moon together / Ethan Long.
Description: First edition. | New York : Henry Holt and Company, 2020. | Series: Happy County ; book 2 | "Christy Ottaviano Books."
Audience: Ages 2–6. | Audience: Grades K–1. | Summary: The animal residents of Happy County
learn about the important activities of the Sun and the Moon.
Identifiers: LCCN 2019039253 | ISBN 9781250191748 (hardcover)
Subjects: CYAC: Sun—Fiction. | Moon—Fiction. | Animals—Fiction.
Classification: LCC PZ7.L8453 Su 2020 | DDC [E]—dc23
LC record available at https://lccn.loc.gov/2019039253

Our books may be purchased in bulk for promotional, educational, or business use. Please contact your local bookseller or the Macmillan
Corporate and Premium Sales Department at (800) 221-7945 ext. 5442 or by email at MacmillanSpecialMarkets@macmillan.com.

First edition, 2020 / Design by Ethan Long
Artwork created with graphite pencil on Strathmore drawing paper, then scanned and colorized digitally.
Printed in China by RR Donnelley Asia Printing Solutions Ltd., Dongguan City, Guangdong Province

1 3 5 7 9 10 8 6 4 2

HAPPY COUNTY

Sun and Moon Together

Ethan Long

Christy Ottaviano Books

HENRY HOLT AND COMPANY

New York

COMB DEPOT

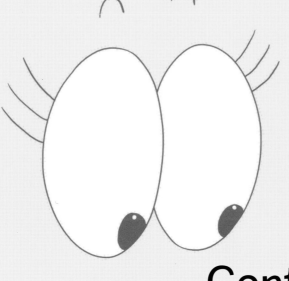

Contents

Welcome................................ 8

Grammy Tammy 10

The Water Cycle 12

Photosynthesis 14

Evening Falls 16

Phases of the Moon.................. 18

Pick a Tide 19

A Moon Movie 20

The Planets 22

Hot-Air Hullabaloo.................... 25

The Bright Brothers................. 26

At the Beach 30

Sssonny's Sssunflowers............ 32

Solar Power........................... 34

Go, Team, Go! 36

Moon Shadows...................... 38

Night Sounds 40

Turn Up the Music! 42

Welcome to another wonderful morning in Happy County! The Sun has risen and is shining down on the bustling landscape.

8

She sees Lucy Livingood sprucing up the landscape,
the County Mounties helping at the crosswalk, and
Hannah the Handywoman repairing an old roof.

antenna

cloud

city

hot dog

Stadium

taxi

FRANK'S

jogger

library

pine
tree

sculpture

dogs

fountain

LIBRARY

BRIDGE
FREEZES
BEFORE
ROAD

bench

building

bush

crosswalk

backpack

school bus

chicken

crane

beams

hard hat

Can you find two friendly dogs?
Do you see a delicious breakfast?
How about a needle in a haystack?
The Sun sees them all.

9

Grammy Tammy

Grammy Tammy is in from Miami.
Daddy and Mommy are out playing rummy.

The laundry is grimy . . .

and slimy . . .

and smells like salami.

It is fumy . . .

and crummy . . .

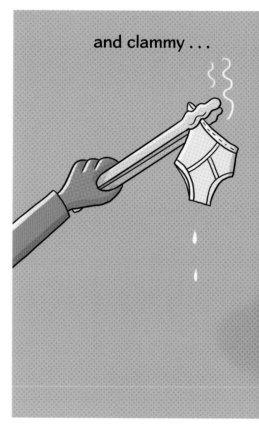

and clammy . . .

The grimy, slimy, fumy, crummy, clammy laundry upsets Grammy Tammy's tummy.

Jimmy! Your laundry is grimy and slimy and smells like salami! It's fumy and crummy and clammy!

But, Grammy Tammy . . .

It's Sammy's!

Gammy!

Grammy Tammy is no dummy.
She leaves the grimy, slimy, fumy, crummy,
clammy laundry for Mommy and Daddy.

The Water Cycle

The Earth's water recycles itself through the water cycle. Here's how it works:

1. Evaporation happens when the Sun heats up water in oceans, rivers, and lakes and turns it into water vapor. The water vapor rises into the air.

2. Condensation occurs when the water vapor cools and forms clouds, where it changes back into liquid.

3. Precipitation happens when the water has condensed so much that the air cannot hold it anymore. The clouds get heavy and the water falls back to Earth in the form of rain, snow, sleet, or hail.

4. Collection occurs when water flows back into oceans, rivers, and lakes. It can also remain on land, where it soaks into the Earth. Plants and animals drink it. Then the water cycle starts all over again!

1. Evaporation → 2. Condensation

4. Collection ← 3. Precipitation

The Sun is an essential part of this process. It makes her happy to see the Earth's water cycling around and around. You should be happy, too!

Photosynthesis

Photosynthesis is how plants eat and breathe. They absorb sunlight, carbon dioxide gas, water, and minerals and turn it all into oxygen (which we breathe) and sugars (which the plant uses to grow). Without photosynthesis, we would not live very long.
The Sun knows this, so she keeps shining brightly.

Evening Falls

As the Sun says goodbye for now, the Moon pops into view.
He has been waiting all day for a fantastic evening of fun!

He sees the Walkers roasting marshmallows.
Mr. and Mrs. Wilson are going on a date
to the movies.
Billy, from Three Guys Pies, is delivering
a pizza.

It looks like it's going to be
an action-packed night!

fire station

fire truck

STATION 59

planetarium

planet

frog

R-IBBIT

campfire

rowboat

pond

bear

creek

cabin

tent

pine
trees

log

mosquito

dock

snake

tulips

aluminum
cans

delivery truck

HAMAZON
PRIME

road

sidewalk

ham

smoke

birdbath

Phases of the Moon

First quarter

Waxing gibbous

Waxing crescent

Full moon

New moon

The Moon likes to make silly faces, depending on his phases, which reflect how the Sun's light is hitting him.

Waning gibbous

Third quarter

Waning crescent

No matter which face or phase he is making, he always adds some personality to the night sky!

Pick a Tide

Rising and falling water levels are called tides.
Tides are due to the gravitational pull of the Sun and
the Moon as well as the rotation of the Earth.
Right now the tide is LOW.

Now the tide is HIGH.
Make sure you don't get stuck underwater.

A Moon Movie

21

The Planets

The Sun is at the center of our solar system, which has eight planets. Each planet has its own climate and characteristics.

Earth

Venus

Mercury

Mars

The farther away from the Sun, the colder the planets are. Earth is the only planet where humans can live, although many people dream of living on Mars.

Jupiter

Uranus

Saturn

Neptune

Waaaaaaaaaaaah! I'm feeling left out!

In the past, Pluto was considered a planet. Now scientists believe it is smaller, a dwarf planet.

Pluto

It's time to take a breather, Moon. You've been out all night! The Sun will take it from here. She's up bright and early, and just in time, too! The morning sunrise is also called dawn.

Hot-Air Hullabaloo

The balloons look beautiful against the glowing sky.
How many designs can you find?

The Bright Brothers

It is a wonderful morning for a flight across the water. Wilbur and Orzo Bright are excited to catch the wind.

Where are we headed today, Orzo?

I can't tell! The Sun is blinding me!

Down . . .
Down . . .
Down go Wilbur and Orzo.

It is dark at the bottom of the ocean.

And it's hard to fix a hot-air balloon
with sand and seaweed.

POOF!

Hmmm.

banner

BROCCOLI BARN

airplane

pelican

seagulls

lifeguard

cloud

palm tree

a creature

pedal cruiser

sandcastle

camera

roof

shower

flip-flop

magazine

book

crab

cooler

metal detector

BEEP BEEP

puddle

hole

headphones

When it's time to go home, make sure you gather all your things. If you're lucky, you can find someone to carry it for you!

TRASH

Sssonny's Sssunflowers

Sssonny Sssnakerton wants to grow sssunflowers.

He sssows the ssseeds.

He sssoaks the sssoil with sssuper ssseed ssspray.

In ssseconds, the ssseeds ssssprout!

BOINK! BOINK! BOINK! BOINK!

Ssspectacular!

Ssstaggering!

Holy sssmokes!

What will Sssonny do with ssso many sssunflowers?

33

Oh yes! Sssunflower ssseeds for sssale! What a sssuper idea, Sssonny! You are sssuch a sssavvy sssalesman!

Solar Power

In Happy County, lots of folks are experimenting with solar power. Solar power is electricity made from the Sun's light. Folks are using solar panels to power their cars, homes, and businesses.

Sssonny's Sssunflower Ssseeds
Sssix Bucks a Sssack!

MEDICAL CENTER

What if EVERYTHING ran on solar power? It could be very good for the environment!

Go, Team, Go!

It's a beautiful night to meet up with the Moon and watch football. It looks like the Stars are going to win the game. TOUCHDOWN!

Look closely at the stars in the sky. Can you find the Little Dipper? Now look at the crowd. Can you see a fan wearing a fuzzy hat? There is also a player on the field with his helmet off. Do you see him?

GO STARS!

HOME
VISITOR

Moon Shadows

Emma and her mom have wanted to camp out in the backyard for a long time, and they're finally doing it. They're calling it "Girls' Night."

Emma makes a moon shadow. It's a bunny rabbit.

Mom makes a cactus.

They team up to make other shadows.
What is this?

And this?

How about this one?

Emma and Mom were having fun, but not
anymore. What in the world is it?!
It's just Ian and Dad trying to be funny.

But Emma and Mom have the last laugh . . . because they locked the door.

Night Sounds

Nighttime noises can sound scary, but if you say them out loud, it makes them sound funny. Go ahead, try it!

MEEEOWWW!

GRRRRRRRR

SSSSSSSSSSS!

SQUEAK SQUEAK!

RATTLE RATTLE!

SKRIIIITCH

CRRROAK! CRRROAK!

BZZZ ZZZZ!

WZZZZZZz!

Turn Up the Music!

That's right! Tonight's the Night Owls concert.
They've already started playing their opening song.
What an exciting night this is going to be!

DRINKS $4.00
PRETZELS $4.00
ICE CREAM $3.00

The Bright Brothers are here.
Sssonny Sssnakerton has a sssuper ssspot.
And of course, the Moon has a front-row seat!

THE NIGHT OWLS

Tomorrow is a new day. If you get up early
enough, you can catch the Sun rising and shining
down on Happy County, just as she always does.
See you soon!

44